Christmas Mouse

Illustrated by Jon Goodell

Published by Sequoia Children's Publishing,
a division of Phoenix International Publications, Inc.

8501 West Higgins Road
Chicago, Illinois 60631

59 Gloucester Place
London W1U 8JJ

© 2021 Sequoia Publishing & Media, LLC

Customer Service: cs@sequoiakidsbooks.com

Sequoia Children's Publishing and associated logo are trademarks and/or
registered trademarks of Sequoia Publishing & Media, LLC.

www.sequoiakidsbooks.com

ISBN 978-1-6426-9140-5

sequoia™
children's publishing

When the wind whips and the snow blows, the country mice know it's time to leave the fields and find a place to live all winter. They pack up nuts, seeds, and their belongings. Then they look for cozy little houses to stay in during the cold winter months.

This is the story of one mouse family and the home they moved into right before Christmas. They made beds of warm straw and sturdy acorns that they could snuggle in.

Papa Mouse was very happy that his family would be warm and comfortable during the snowy winter.

The family settled into a comfortable routine in their new home. Mama Mouse spent most nights knitting scarves and sweaters for her family while the three mouse children scampered around the house.

One night, Papa Mouse peered outside and announced, "Look at all the Christmas lights. It's almost time for Santa to arrive."

Mama Mouse replied, "Oh, yes, I've smelled all those fresh chestnuts roasting over the fires."

"And those yummy gingerbread men," added Papa.

Late one night, Papa Mouse noticed that stockings had been hung for each member of the family.

"What's this?" he asked.

Mama Mouse looked at Papa Mouse and said, "I am getting ready for our Christmas celebration. Our children have been very good and deserve some special gifts."

Papa scratched his head. "What if Santa can't find us in our new home?"

Mama answered, "Oh, he will find us, Papa. You just need to think good thoughts and believe in Santa Claus. And we are going to do just that!"

Christmas Eve finally arrived. The mouse children were so excited about Santa Claus that they tossed and turned in their little bed. They had visions of cheese bits, toys, and little sugarplums dancing all around in their heads.

Papa said to Mama Mouse, "I just hope you're right about Santa." He did not want his children to be disappointed on Christmas morning.

"Don't worry," Mama replied confidently. "He'll be here."

She took a few fresh-baked cookies to leave by the tree for Santa Claus. Papa followed her. He was still worried.

"How will Santa find five mice tucked away in a new house?" Papa wondered.

"Trust me, Papa," Mama said. "Santa is going to find us. I'm sure he knows where all the world's creatures live."

Mama glanced over at the pretty tree that she had worked so hard to decorate. She said to Papa, "We can't forget who takes Santa to all these places. Our forest friends, the reindeer."

Papa looked at the beautiful tree and saw that it was filled with treats their reindeer friends enjoyed. There were candy canes, popcorn, and even wrapped carrots for the reindeer!

Mama Mouse said, "And remember that Dancer is on Santa's reindeer team this year. He called her up to sleigh duty in the North Pole this past fall."

"Yes, I remember that," said Papa.

"Did you tell her we were moving to a new house?" said Papa.

"Of course," replied Mama.

Papa looked outside just in time to see Dancer and the other reindeer.

Soon there was the sound of reindeer hooves clattering on the roof. Then Mama and Papa Mouse heard Santa Claus making his way down the chimney. He discovered the snack from Mama and Papa. Santa enjoyed the cold milk and ate all the cookies!

When they heard him rustling around the tree, they both jumped into bed. They did not want to spoil Santa's Christmas Eve surprise!

Santa slipped some packages under the tree. He shushed the talking doll and took some treats for his reindeer before heading up the chimney.

Santa returned to the sleigh and his team of reindeer. Mama and Papa Mouse heard loud crunching sounds up on the rooftop. They were glad that they had thought to leave crispy carrots and other treats for their friend Dancer and the rest of the reindeer.

Papa leaned his head out the window and saw Santa turn his sleigh around.

"Thank you, Santa. Thank you, Dancer. Thanks, everyone," said Papa.

Santa Claus and his team of reindeer flew away. Papa Mouse was so happy to see Santa wink and wave at him.

After Papa Mouse finished saying his thanks to Santa and the reindeer, Papa scurried downstairs to see what Santa had left under the tree.

He was not disappointed. Santa had filled the stockings with cheese and other treats. He also left the children a talking doll, a train set, and even a shiny metal robot!

Papa was so excited that he decided to head to the forest to wish everyone a very merry Christmas. He tied a scarf around his neck and dashed outside. Papa hoped to spread some holiday cheer to all his dear friends!

When Papa Mouse arrived at the forest, he found that Santa had brought his friends all sorts of wonderful gifts and tasty treats to eat.

Mama Mouse had been right all along. As long as you believe in Santa, he will bring the joy of Christmas to you... no matter where you live.